Since its creation in 1962 by Stan Lee,
the adventures of Peter Parker as his web-slinging
alias, Spider-Man, have amassed phenomenal success.
Now one of the most recognisable Super Heroes in
the world, and with adaptations across all platforms,
The Amazing Spider-Man is just that… amazing!

Autumn
Publishing

Published in 2019
by Autumn Publishing
Cottage Farm
Sywell
NN6 0BJ
www.igloobooks.com

Autumn is an imprint of Bonnier Books UK

© 2019 MARVEL

LEO002 0419
2 4 6 8 10 9 7 5 3 1
ISBN 978-1-78905-848-2

Printed and manufactured in China

Autumn
Publishing

Contents

The Story of Spider-Man

Peter Parker was just your average teenager from Queens, New York. He lived with his Aunt May and Uncle Ben and he attended Midtown High. Peter was very studious and was considered one of the smartest kids in school. Unfortunately, his good grades didn't make him very popular with some of his classmates.

Flash Thompson, the school bully, regularly tormented Peter. One day, Flash pushed him to the ground and Peter's books and papers scattered everywhere. "Hey, Parker, you dropped your books," Flash sneered.

School was tough for Peter, but he was always happy at home. Aunt May and Uncle Ben loved Peter completely. Uncle Ben always reminded Peter that he was going to do something special with his life.

"You are incredibly smart, Peter," Aunt May said. "You have the ability to be anything you want to be."

"Well, actually, I was thinking that I might want to be a scientist someday," Peter replied.

Uncle Ben put his arm round Peter. "A scientist is a very important job. Science is power. And remember – with great power comes great responsibility."

Then, one day Peter's life changed while he was on a school trip to the Science Hall. He was excited to see real-life scientists at work. But while Peter looked round at the exhibits, a spider passed through radioactive waves. Peter was so distracted, he didn't notice the radioactive spider head right towards him.

At that moment, the radioactive spider bit Peter! He could never have imagined what an impact this one bite would have on his life. Peter Parker would never be the same again.

Before Peter knew it, he had adopted many characteristics of a spider. He could cling to walls, he was superstrong and he also had spider-sense. This meant that Peter experienced a strong tingling feeling that alerted him to danger. These skills made Peter extremely powerful.

Peter wanted to keep his new identity a secret, so he stayed up all night creating a spider-suit and mask. He even stitched a large spider on the front of it.

Peter also worked hard to figure out how to control his new powers. Using his vast knowledge of science, he made web-shooters and practised shooting them in his bedroom. Peter's superstrong webs stuck to every surface. Soon, his entire room was covered in webs! *Okay, so it's not as easy as it looks*, Peter thought.

Like all teenagers, Peter wanted to make money. He needed a job where he could use his powers to his advantage. So, Peter became a wrestler. "Please welcome to the ring… Spider-Man!" the announcer would boom.

Peter used his powers to defeat every opponent. One night, Peter noticed the wrestling gym was being robbed. Peter didn't care and the robber ended up getting away.

When Peter got home later that night, he saw police cars in front of his house. He raced inside and found out that someone had attacked and hurt Uncle Ben. Aunt May and Peter were devastated.

The police officers told Peter not to worry because they had the criminal cornered at an old warehouse. But Peter knew he had to take matters into his own hands.

Peter put on his Spider-Man suit and swung through the city. He was determined to avenge Uncle Ben.

At last, Peter arrived at the warehouse. The thief was stunned as he watched Spider-Man in action. Spider-Man shot a web and trapped the crook. After getting a good look at him, Spider-Man realised that it was the same criminal he had watched escape from the wrestling gym.

If only I had stopped him then! he thought. Peter vowed that from then on he would help others whenever it was in his power. He would never let anything like this happen again.

Just one month earlier, Peter would have been busy studying for his chemistry exam like any normal teenager, but everything had changed. He might still have to do homework from time to time, but Peter was also Spider-Man.

The next day at school, everyone couldn't stop talking about Spider-Man.

"I think he's great," Flash said, as he looked at an article about the new hero. "He's just trying to help the city."

Peter smiled. If only Flash knew who Peter really was!

The next day, Spider-Man heard about another criminal on the loose in Manhattan. Spider-Man swung down to confront the villain, who he discovered had the ability to control electricity. It was Electro! The hero used his web-shooters, and after a few tries, the Super Villain was defeated.

In that moment, Spider-Man realised something. It was his destiny to always protect others, and if he worked hard enough, maybe one day he could become a great Super Hero. Spider-Man thought back to the words that Uncle Ben always used to say: With great power comes great responsibility.

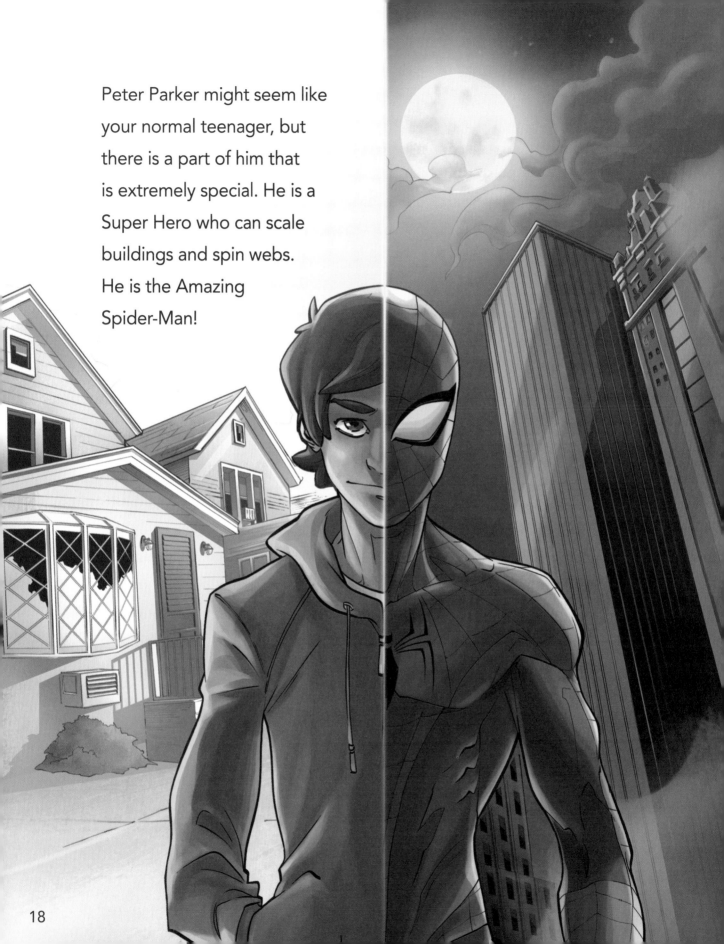

Peter Parker might seem like your normal teenager, but there is a part of him that is extremely special. He is a Super Hero who can scale buildings and spin webs. He is the Amazing Spider-Man!

Reptile Rampage!

Dr. Curtis Connors, also known as the Lizard, was in trouble. Peter Parker knew it as soon as he saw all the pictures of the Lizard splashed across the front page of the Daily Bugle. Peter also knew that his boss, J. Jonah Jameson, would be mad that Peter hadn't delivered exclusive pictures of the Lizard.

As soon as Peter walked into the Daily Bugle, J. Jonah Jameson called him into his office. "Parker, the Lizard is on the loose and I need pictures," he demanded. "I don't care if you have to camp out in a swamp. I want a shot for the front page. And I also want a picture of Spider-Man fighting the Lizard!" JJJ shouted.
He always expected perfection.

"I'm your man. I'll get you those shots," Peter told his boss.

Meanwhile, Dr. Connors's wife, Martha, was very upset. She noticed her husband mixing up a strange formula earlier that week. She knew that he was trying to create a serum that would help him grow back his missing arm, but she also knew that it came with a serious side effect. It turned Dr. Connors into an evil villain called the Lizard!

Spider-Man found Martha Connors sitting on her porch. She was looking at a picture of her husband. "I wish he didn't care about growing back that arm."

She looked at Spider-Man with concern.

"I'll find him," Spidey told her. "Don't worry."

"Please hurry," Mrs. Connors said. "You need to bring him to the lab and feed him the antidote."

"Got it! He won't be a lawless lizard much longer. Soon he will be back to being good old Dr. Connors."

Spidey searched New York City up and down. Finally, he spotted the Lizard. Spider-Man chased him into an ice cream shop, hoping to lock the cold-blooded beast in a freezer, which would diminish the Lizard's strength. Unfortunately for Peter, the Lizard escaped!

"I'm not a fan of frozen treatsss," the Lizard called out to Spidey.

"If you try to run from me, you're going to be on a rocky road," Spidey taunted.

The Lizard stomped through the streets, creating a wave of destruction, crushing car windows and damaging shopfronts.

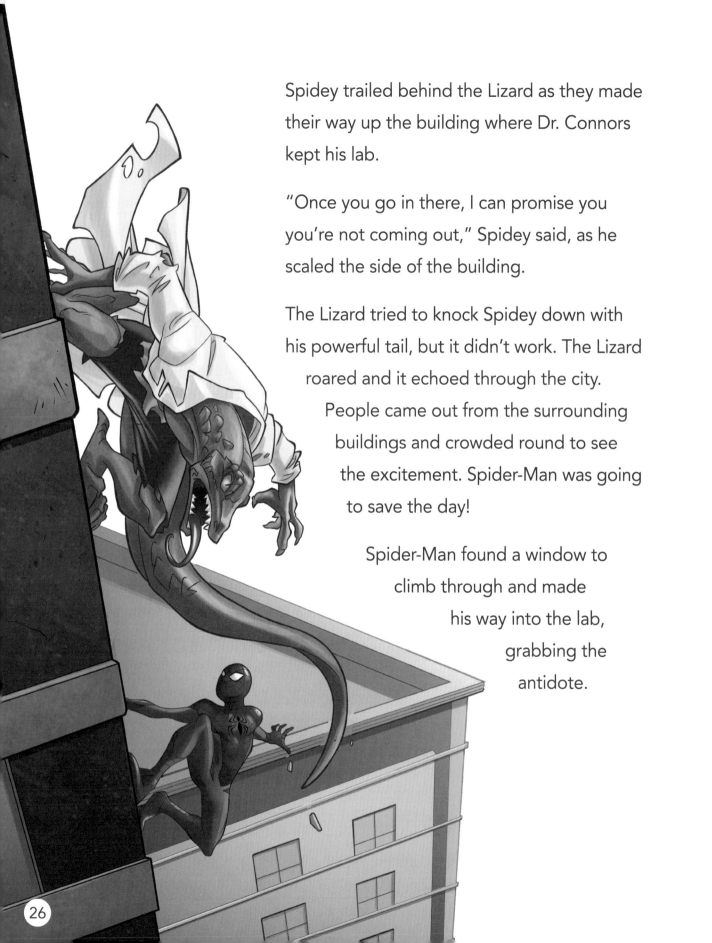

Spidey trailed behind the Lizard as they made their way up the building where Dr. Connors kept his lab.

"Once you go in there, I can promise you you're not coming out," Spidey said, as he scaled the side of the building.

The Lizard tried to knock Spidey down with his powerful tail, but it didn't work. The Lizard roared and it echoed through the city. People came out from the surrounding buildings and crowded round to see the excitement. Spider-Man was going to save the day!

Spider-Man found a window to climb through and made his way into the lab, grabbing the antidote.

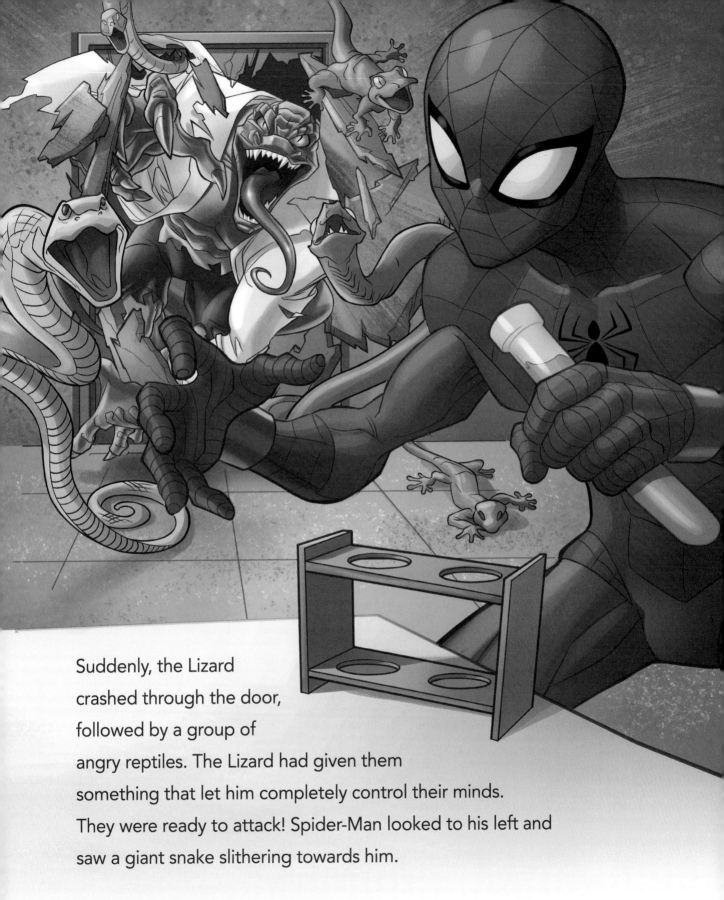

Suddenly, the Lizard
crashed through the door,
followed by a group of
angry reptiles. The Lizard had given them
something that let him completely control their minds.
They were ready to attack! Spider-Man looked to his left and
saw a giant snake slithering towards him.

"Yikes!" Spider-Man shouted, as the monstrous snake coiled itself round his leg. Spidey quickly fired webs at the Lizard as more and more reptiles attacked.

The Lizard dodged Spider-Man's webs and swung his enormous tail. Spidey flew through the air, crashing straight into the lab table. But Spider-Man kept firing his webs! He didn't know if he was going to be able to fight both the Lizard and the cold-blooded fiends.

Spider-Man was in full battle mode with the reptiles when the Lizard threw a desk at him.

"Whoa, bad lizard!" Spidey called out. "Dr. Connors, do you realise what you are doing? You have to stop the Lizard!" But it was pointless. Dr. Connors had no control once the Lizard was unleashed. There was no use reasoning with a monster.

In between fighting, Spidey eyed the antidote. The Lizard used the opportunity to unleash his final attack. He ordered the reptiles to hold Spidey down as he began to strike him over and over. Spider-Man fought back hard, making sure not to bump into the antidote. Finally, Spidey broke free, grabbed the antidote and poured it into the Lizard's open jaws.

Within seconds, the Lizard began to morph until he slowly became Dr. Connors again. Spider-Man was relieved to see the doctor's familiar face.

"Wow, what happened?" Dr. Connors asked.

"It's a long story," Spidey sighed.

Soon, Martha Connors had her husband back and J. Jonah Jameson had his front-page story. Everyone was happy!

That night, Peter came home to one of Aunt May's amazing home-cooked meals. "How was your day, Peter?" Aunt May asked.

Peter didn't even know where to begin. Aunt May didn't know Peter was Spider-Man, and he certainly couldn't tell her about his fight with the Lizard.

"Don't forget to save room for dessert, Peter," Aunt May said, as Peter finished his dinner. "I picked up a pint of ice cream. Your favourite, rocky road."

Seeing Spots

It was a wonderfully sunny day. Peter Parker and Gwen Stacy were strolling through Central Park about to buy hot dogs from a vending cart. "Ketchup, mustard and relish?" Peter asked.

"You know me too well, Parker," Gwen said, smiling. Peter reached into his pocket to pay for the hot dogs when Gwen reached for her purse. "My treat," she said.

Before Peter could argue, a strange black circle appeared below Gwen's purse. The friends were shocked when a white arm covered in black spots came shooting out of the hole. It grabbed Gwen's purse!

Another circle appeared above them. Inside, a man's head emerged.

A menacing voice erupted from the circle. "What a lovely bag. I'm sorry, but I don't believe there will be any hot dogs today."

As suddenly as they appeared, the thief and his black circles disappeared. Gwen was shocked. Peter's eyes narrowed. He was not going to let some freaky villain ruin his perfect day with Gwen. "Wait here!" Peter exclaimed. Before Gwen could say anything, Peter bolted out of sight.

Peter ducked into an alley and changed into his Spider-Man suit to chase down the thief. He had been reading about this polka-dotted villain in the paper – a robber they called the Spot!

Swinging high, Spider-Man looked out over the streets of New York for signs of the criminal. "Ha! I spot you!" he chuckled, as he saw black circles appear beside another potential victim. He swung off to face his foe.

Spider-Man managed to grab the purse with
his web before the Spot could snatch it. "I think
you've collected enough for one day, Spot."

"Spider-Man! I've been waiting to run into you," the Spot
said. "Over and over."

Suddenly, black circles appeared all around Spidey. Out of
them came fists, hitting Spider-Man as the Spot appeared
and reappeared in different directions. The villain was so
fast that even Spider-Man's spider-sense couldn't keep up.

Spider-Man fell, beaten by the Spot. The teleporting villain appeared over him, laughing. "Better luck next time, Bug-Brain!" the Spot taunted, vanishing into thin air.

Feeling woozy, Spidey realised he was going to need some help defeating this new menace. Fortunately, he knew just who to call.

Spidey swung to an abandoned church, hoping this was still the place his friends used as a hideout.

"If anyone can help me, it'll be these two," he muttered, knowing he was running out of options. The Spot was going to be hard to defeat.

Although they had only teamed up a few times before, and one of the two could be kind of creepy, Spider-Man knew he could trust this duo to help him get the job done.

"Cloak! Dagger! Man, am I glad to see you guys," Spider-Man said, as he entered the church. He quickly filled them in on his encounter with the Spot.

"I need your help." Spidey turned to Cloak. "I know you're used to popping in and out of thin air, too."

"I have felt someone tapping into my teleportation force recently," Cloak noted. "It seems this Spot and I share a connection through multiple dimensions."

That gave Dagger an idea. "If we can follow the energy Cloak is feeling, it could lead us to the Spot. Then, my light daggers could help trap him there by draining his energy."

With the plan set, the heroes dived into the darkness of Cloak's cape and disappeared.

When the trio reappeared, they found themselves in the Spot's secret hideout. It was filled with all the stolen purses, jewels and other items the thief had taken on his crime spree.

"Spider-Man! How did you find me here? And who are these freaks?" the Spot asked, shocked.

Spider-Man just smiled. "Looks like you're not the only disappearing act in town, Spot."

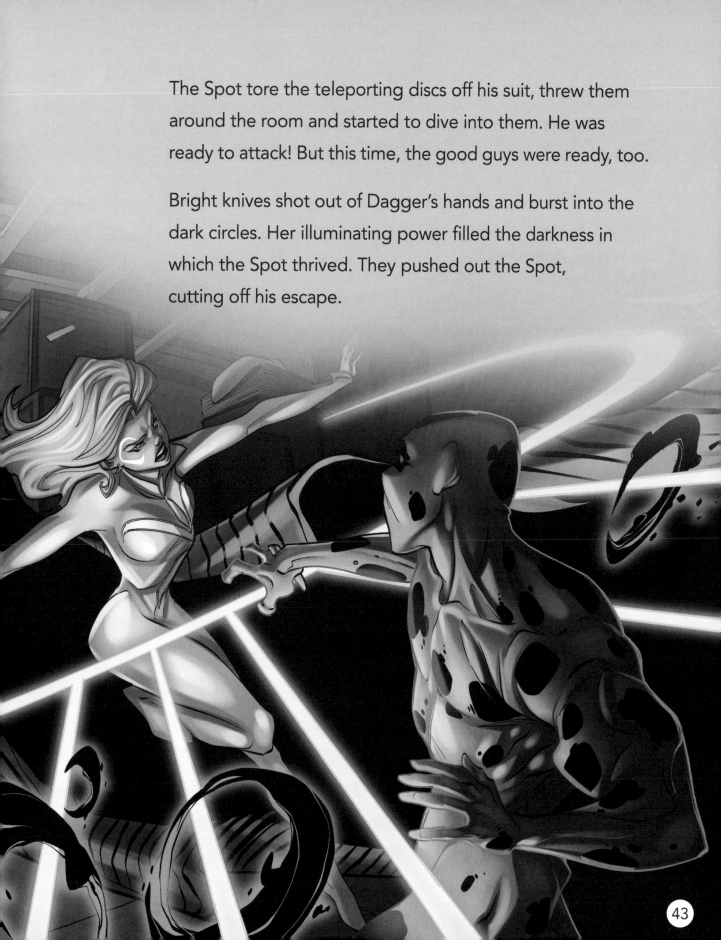

The Spot tore the teleporting discs off his suit, threw them around the room and started to dive into them. He was ready to attack! But this time, the good guys were ready, too.

Bright knives shot out of Dagger's hands and burst into the dark circles. Her illuminating power filled the darkness in which the Spot thrived. They pushed out the Spot, cutting off his escape.

Spider-Man quickly webbed the villain before he could try his teleportation tricks again. "Hmm, looks like you're stuck. I guess you could say my webs are spot-on!"

Dagger chuckled at Spider-Man's bad joke, while Cloak's icy stare never wavered. Their plan worked! The Spot's thieving days were over.

The heroes helped return the stolen items. As the pile grew smaller, Spidey recognised one of the purses and grabbed it.

"Not enough pockets in your suit?" Dagger asked with a wink.

"Hey, bad jokes are my thing," Spider-Man replied. Then, with a quiet whoosh, Cloak whisked Dagger and the Spot away.

Back in Central Park, Peter Parker came running back to Gwen. There was a police officer handing over her purse. "Gwen! You got it back!" Peter exclaimed.

"It was incredible, Peter! Spider-Man caught the thief and brought all the stolen items back. Including my purse."

Peter blushed. "Wow, he's a real hero."

"But you are just as brave, Peter," Gwen said, hugging her friend. "Thanks for looking out for me."

Peter grinned. "I'm sorry I couldn't do more."

"Well," Gwen said, handing the hot dog vendor money, "you certainly did enough to earn this hot dog. My treat, as promised."

"You're the best," Peter said, as he chewed. "Wow, this really hits the spot."

The Amazing Incredible Spider-Hulk

Spider-Man and the Avengers were having dinner at a restaurant after they battled Ultron in Central Park. As the heroes ate, Iron Man challenged Hulk to an arm-wrestling contest. But Iron Man's armoured gauntlets were no match for the Hulk.

"Hulk strong. Too easy," Hulk said.

Spider-Man was a little jealous of his big green pal. *I'm strong, but I'm not Hulk strong*, he thought. *If I could do everything the Hulk can do, I'd be the perfect Super Hero!*

Outside the restaurant, Spider-Man watched as a little girl shyly tugged at the Hulk's trouser leg. "Excuse me," she mumbled. "Will you sign my autograph book?"

The green Avenger nodded graciously. But when he grabbed the pencil, he accidentally crushed it. Spidey could see that the Hulk was upset. He approached Hulk as the disappointed girl walked away.

"Hey, big guy, why the frown?" Spidey asked. Spider-Man was surprised to hear that the Hulk sometimes wanted to be, as he put it, 'more puny, like Bug-Man'.

"Isn't that something," Spider-Man began. "I was just thinking about how sometimes I'd rather be more like you!" Just then, they received an important message from S.H.I.E.L.D.. Nick Fury was unveiling an important new invention!

At S.H.I.E.L.D. headquarters, everyone saw Nick Fury standing next to a high-tech device capped by an enormous purple gemstone. Fury explained that they were there to witness a demonstration of a machine that would allow two Super Heroes to temporarily swap abilities. This way, they could catch Super Villains off guard.

Spidey and the Hulk couldn't believe what they were hearing. It would be like switching places! When Fury asked for volunteers, two hands immediately went up: a big green one and a smaller red one.

Spider-Man and the Hulk stood side by side over a big red X on the floor. Fury activated the device. The machine started to hum and the purple gemstone glowed. It shot out a beam, covering both the Hulk and Spider-Man.

But the machine overheated, causing an explosion that shook the room! When the smoke cleared, everyone stared at the figure standing on the red X. It wasn't Spidey. It wasn't the Hulk. It looked like both of them… combined! Two heroes had merged into one hybrid creature – the Spider-Hulk!

Peering at Iron Man's armour, Spider-Hulk studied his reflection in its gleaming surface. The face that stared back at him was familiar, and yet… unfamiliar. Confused and frustrated, Spider-Hulk couldn't control his feelings. "Bug-Hulk SMASH!" he yelled, pounding his fists into the floor.

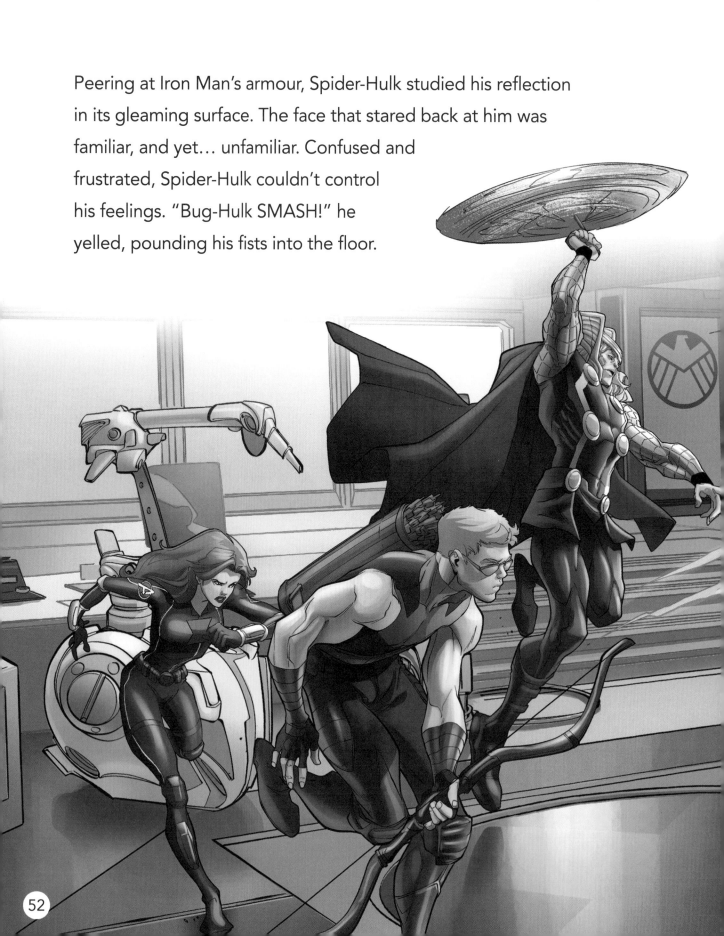

Captain America tried to calm down the heroic hybrid. "At ease, soldier!" Cap shouted over the noise. But before he could continue, Spider-Hulk grabbed Cap's shield and flung it into the wall. Then, the frightened Spider-Hulk turned and crashed through the glass window. The Avengers raced after him.

Spider-Hulk couldn't think clearly. It felt as though there were two separate voices in his head! He just wanted to get away from the people trying to capture him. He didn't realise his pursuers were his friends, the Avengers. "Bug-Hulk's bug-sense tingling," he muttered to himself.

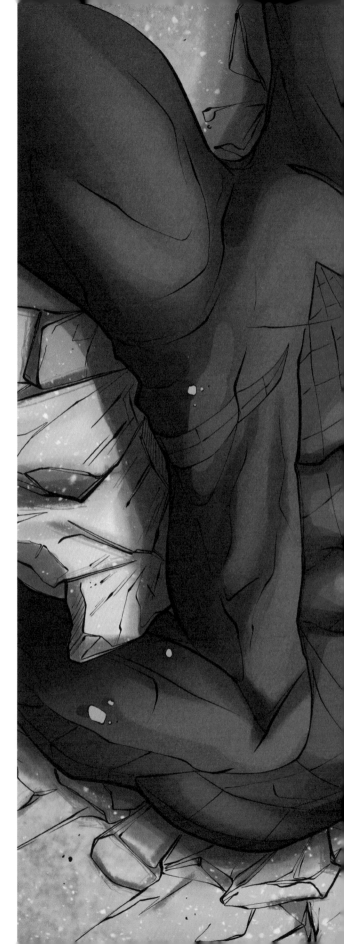

Spider-Hulk tried using his webbing to outrun the Avengers, but when he attempted to swing away, his body twisted awkwardly in the air. The web-line snapped and Spider-Hulk fell, smashing into the pavement below!

With Spider-Hulk momentarily weakened, Hawkeye quickly came up with a plan. He had sometimes calmed the Hulk down with a nursery rhyme, so he sat down and began reading to Spider-Hulk. It worked too well. The hybrid hero thought it was bedtime and he fled looking for a midnight snack!

This gave Black Widow an idea. The Avengers would draw Spider-Hulk back to S.H.I.E.L.D. headquarters using the one thing both Spider-Man and the Hulk love: food! When Thor and Black Widow found Spider-Hulk, he was ransacking every hot dog cart in the city looking for snacks. Thor stood in his path and tried to lure Spider-Hulk away with a delicious chocolate cake from the bakery.

But before Thor could lead the way back to headquarters, Spider-Hulk swallowed the entire cake. The new Super Hero also had a super appetite!

Iron Man knew that Spider-Man was really Peter Parker, a teenager who couldn't resist his Aunt May's famous wheat cakes. So, the armoured Avenger instructed his personal chef to make enough wheat cakes to feed a small country. In other words, enough wheat cakes to feed one Spider-Hulk.

Iron Man zoomed around the city, leaving a trail of wheat cakes for his fused friend to follow. It worked! The Spider-Hulk gobbled each tasty treat, leading him closer and closer to the device that caused all this chaos in the first place.

Spider-Hulk was so busy wolfing down wheat cakes, he didn't notice he was sitting on the big red X. He swallowed the last piece of wheat cake and said, "Spider-Hulk wants maple—" But before he could finish his sentence, Nick Fury pressed the reverse button. Once again, the purple gemstone glowed and Spider-Hulk was shot with an energy beam.

When the light faded, two heroes stepped forth: Spider-Man and the Hulk!

"I really learnt something today," Spider-Man told the Hulk. "I used to think I wanted to be more like you. But being Spider-Hulk just… didn't feel like me. And I like being me."

The green goliath nodded. "Hulk learnt something, too," he began. "Hulk learnt that Bug-Man's puny costume is bad fit on Hulk-size body!"

The two friends laughed. Then, they patted their bellies and turned to the other Avengers. "Okay," Spider-Man said with a wink, "who's up for some dessert?"

The Hunt for Black Panther

Kraven the Hunter loved to hunt wild animals. The only thing he loved more than hunting was the fame that came along with it. But one day, after Kraven had captured a pair of cheetahs, he didn't feel the same sense of accomplishment he normally felt after a successful hunt.

Kraven hungered for a new prey that would give him a real challenge. But where could he find such a foe?

A few days later, Peter Parker was sent by the Daily Bugle to photograph the annual Protection of Endangered Animals conference in Upper Manhattan. Giving the keynote speech was none other than T'Challa, ruler of the African nation of Wakanda.

Peter was excited for the chance to actually see T'Challa speak. The king was a compassionate ruler and a scientific genius.

But T'Challa had a secret. He was also the Super Hero Black Panther!

"In order to protect the animals of Earth," the king began, "it is our duty to fight back against illegal hunters and poachers."

Black Panther protected his nation and its animal kingdom from villains by using his superhuman strength, speed and agility. One of those villains was Kraven the Hunter.

Desperate for a new challenge, Kraven knew that this conference was the perfect place to find his next prey – Black Panther! The villain burst through the window in a spray of broken glass.

"T'Challa!" he bellowed. "I request a meeting with the Black Panther."

T'Challa's eyes narrowed. "Black Panther will never bow to the likes of you!"

Kraven smirked. "I assumed there would be some protest… which is why I brought some backup!"

Just then, Kraven let out a high-pitched whistle and two cheetahs leapt down from the window above! "No one here is allowed to leave until the Black Panther is mine!"

In the chaos, Peter Parker's spider-senses were tingling like crazy. Peter knew he had to act fast. This place was turning into a zoo!

Meanwhile, T'Challa's bodyguards, the
Dora Milaje, attempted to move the
Wakandan king to safety.

"Save your energy," he commanded.
"It's time for Black Panther to strike."

Black Panther turned round to discover he had been joined by Spider-Man!

"What are you doing here?" Black Panther asked.

"Nice to see you, too," Spider-Man said, as he fired a ball of web fluid at the nearest cheetah. "Stand back! I've beaten Kraven before. I can deal with these overgrown house cats."

"Spider-Man, no! You must be careful!" Black Panther tried to warn the web-slinger, but it was already too late.

"Whoa! Nice kitty!" Spider-Man exclaimed, as the cheetah grabbed his web and lunged towards him.

Acting fast, Black Panther grabbed the cheetah before Spider-Man was harmed. "Listen to me. My animal instincts tell me that these creatures are being held here against their will. They will only attack you if they are provoked."

But Spidey wasn't out of danger yet! Kraven threw a spear at the web-slinger, but Spidey rolled out of the way just in time!

"I'll calm them down while you get Kraven," Black Panther said to Spidey.

"On it!" Spider-Man said, as he swung towards the balcony.

While holding back the cheetahs, Black Panther massaged the backs of their heads. Kraven had found a way to increase the aggression of these animals. Luckily, Black Panther was more familiar with wildlife. He safely pressed down on the cheetahs' pressure points to relax the animals' anger.

"That should calm you down," he said, petting the cheetahs.

With the cheetahs under control, Spider-Man caught up with the villainous hunter.

"You are nothing but a minor nuisance. I did not come here for you, but if I must capture you, too, so be it!" Kraven said. He began throwing knives at the web-slinging hero. Unfortunately for Kraven, Spidey's trusty spider-sense made it impossible for him to land an attack.

"What's the matter, Kraven?" Spider-Man asked. "Can't catch a little spider?"

"Maybe it would help if you took care of that smell first, Kraven. P-U! Or do they not have showers in the jungle?" Spider-Man joked.

Blinded with anger, Kraven was unable to focus on the fight with the two Super Heroes. Spider-Man quickly used his web-shooters to disarm Kraven, giving Black Panther the perfect opening for an attack.

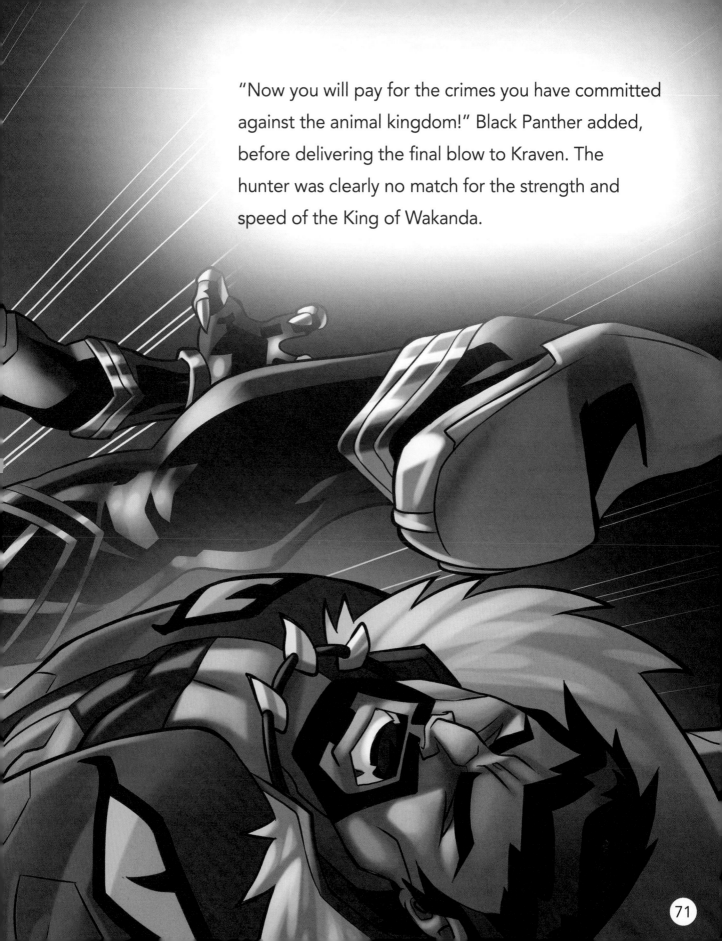

"Now you will pay for the crimes you have committed against the animal kingdom!" Black Panther added, before delivering the final blow to Kraven. The hunter was clearly no match for the strength and speed of the King of Wakanda.

Kraven was finally defeated.

"Beaten by a spider and a cat," Kraven mumbled.

"What's wrong? Don't like being held in captivity?" Spider-Man asked.

Black Panther addressed the crowd of frightened spectators. "You are all safe! These majestic creatures are not the enemy. They deserve respect and compassion. And thank you, Spider-Man, for helping me save them."

Spider-Man was caught off guard by the Black Panther's kind words. "Wow. Thanks, Black Panther. Now might not be a good time, but do you mind if we take a selfie?"